Willi...
and the
Hounds of Gobbolot

Willie wasn't worried about himself, of course.

But he was worried about Sally.

The Hounds of Gobbolot were near now. Their eyes became bigger and bluer and began to twirl round. Willie couldn't help noticing their teeth were like those long needles dentists shove in your gums.

"How are you doing with the boy creature, Claud?" said the Hound named Cecil. "Are you in control of his m ind yet?"

"I seem to be encountering slight opposition."

That was putting it mildly. Willie was fighting with every fibre of his superhuman powers to stay awake. In the last few seconds the pale, unhappy features of his Uncle Rumpus seemed to have loomed up in his head. I am extremely brainy and therefore know what is best for you, *his uncle's voice kept saying.* Sleep now. Let me take charge.

Willie struggled hard against the voice but with every second that passed his willpower weakened.

Willie Scrimshaw
and the
Hounds of Gobbolot

Dick Cate (signature)

Dick Cate
Illustrated by John Eastwood

Lions
An Imprint of HarperCollinsPublishers

To my gransdon
Eldon Cate

First published in Great Britain in Lions in 1993
Lions is an imprint of HarperCollins Children's Books,
a division of HarperCollins Publishers Ltd, 77-85 Fulham Palace
Road, Hammersmith, London W6 8JB

Text copyright © Dick Cate 1993
Illustrations copyright © John Eastwood 1993

ISBN 0 00 674651 9

Printed and bound in Great Britain
by HarperCollins Book Manufacturing Ltd, Glasgow

ONE

Something Funny in the Coal House

"There's something funny in our coal house, Our Dad," said Willie's sister Darleen when she got home on Saturday night.

"It'll be next-door's cat," said Mr Scrimshaw looking up from his *Muckyford Daily Lyre*. "It's always trying to do its business in there."

"It's not a cat, Dad!" said Darleen as she

hung up her coat and squeezed past her mam in their small back kitchen.

"How do you know, Our Darleen?" asked Mrs Scrimshaw who was chopping up chips for their supper. "Has Wayne been upsetting you again?"

"No, Mam, he hasn't!" said Darleen, her eyes close to tears.

Until last week she and her boyfriend Wayne had been perfectly happy practising the tango, et cetera, in her bedroom, but now he had taken the ring from his nose and was talking of removing the tints from his hair. It had their Darleen all het up.

"And I *know* it isn't a cat," she said, "because I opened the coal-house door and looked in. There's a right funny article in there. It keeps spinning round with a bit of paper in its hand."

"It'll be the postman," said her dad. He lit up his pipe. "I expect he's been to the Club for a couple of pints."

"It's not the postman, Dad. It's even

2

funnier looking. It has a right big nose and skinny legs."

"That sounds like Our Willie," said Mr Scrimshaw.

"It's not me, Dad. I'm here," said Willie, who all this time had been sitting next to his dad on their busted sofa studying his nine times table because Miss Minsky was giving them a test on Monday.

"You're quite right, lad," said Mr Scrimshaw lowering his paper and looking down at him. "I never noticed you sitting there."

It was no wonder, really. Small, skinny and with not too much to say for himself, Willie Scrimshaw was one of those kids easily overlooked. Miss Minsky had once marked him absent when he was feeding the class hamster: she'd failed to see him against the bars of the cage.

"I wish you'd go out and have a look, Dad," said Darleen. "Whatever it is has this blue flickering light all round it and keeps shouting *Jeepio!*"

"I *told* you it was the postman!" said Mr Scrimshaw.

"It isn't the postman, Dad! Will you go out and have a look?"

"Don't bother, Dad," said Willie, already on his way. "I'll do it."

"Good lad, Willie," said his mam as he went through the back kitchen. "And wipe that lump of marmalade off your specs first and you might be able to see better. I've saved you some titbits for Mr Fletcher's pig and horse tomorrow."

"Thanks a lot, Mam," said Willie as he went out.

TWO

Entangled in Bloomers

Willie Scrimshaw was helpful and kind, and not only to people. He was always rescuing lost frogs and finding holes for homeless worms. Every night, after tea, he took tasty scraps down to Mr Fletcher's pig, Perce, and his old horse, Samantha, who lived in the allotments.

But this time there was more to it than being helpful.

The fact was – despite appearances – Willie Scrimshaw was a creature of super-human powers, a prince from the faraway planet of Burp. He was disguised to look like an ordinary kid and wore jam-jar specs to conceal his X-ray eyes. His mission on Earth was to keep Law and Order. Last term he had stopped robbers pinching the school money for the Blind Dogs' Appeal. At the mention of Jeepio his quick brain had swung into action, for Jeepio was the Royal

5

Messenger from his home planet. No doubt he was bringing news of another important mission.

After he had closed the back door behind him he stood for a moment looking up at the stars, wondering what his other mam and dad were doing up on Burp.

Probably signing royal bits of paper while they were waited on hand and foot by jet-propelled robots.

Coming down to earth a little, Willie wondered how Shrimp Salmon was getting on. Shrimp Salmon, his best pal, had gone down to the limestone quarry that night to join Reggie Flagg's gang for fighting the Bottom Enders. They were always arguing about who owned the council rubbish tip. Willie had almost gone with him but in the end he hadn't.

Not because he was scared. Willie wasn't scared of anything. It was just that he longed for the day when there was peace and quiet all over and the worst bit on the news was the England soccer results. He also longed for the day when Sally Mow fancied him, which didn't seem likely at the moment because she was doting on Nathan Peabody who was good at playing the trumpet.

Life indeed seemed grim down here on

Earth, but as he crossed the back yard Willie determined to keep his mind on higher things. As a result, he found himself entangled in his mam's bloomers fluttering on the clothesline and then whammed his nose on her brand-new clothes prop.

Other folk might have been put off by this. But not Willie. If you were of noble blood and your true name was Prince Dingbat Bogholler you had to have lofty visions, even if every now and then you ended up entangled in bloomers. He often dreamed of rescuing fair maidens on a gallant white charger. All the maidens looked exactly like Sally Mow slightly disguised under a wimple (or was it a womple? He wasn't right cracky on details).

The fact was, most folk couldn't see further than their noses but Willie was always looking forward to a time when the factories stopped belching smoke and pollution. Everybody would probably grow coconuts instead and go around wearing next-to-nowt because somebody had improved the climate. Even in Muckyford it would be like being at the seaside every day.

Then he yanked open the coal-house door and looked in.

THREE

A Message From Outer Spice

"Where the duckens have *you* been?" said Jeepio. "I've been waiting here for odges."

"Who's Hodges?" asked Willie.

"I am not refereeing to a person. It is a lingth of tim."

"Oh, I see," said Willie. "I'm right sorry."

He hardly recognised the Royal Messenger. Indeed, he could hardly see him. Only his eyes stared out of the darkness.

"Where the dibble am I?" snapped Jeepio.

"In our coal hole. Good job you didn't land next door."

"Why?"

"That's our outside bog. My mam only cleans it when Aunty Flora comes."

"We have no tim for truffles," said Jeepio. By now Willie could see his nose – long, quivering and with bristles at the end, like an irritated bottle-brush. "Your nobble father sends his grottings."

"Same here," said Willie. "How's my mam?"

"She sends you her bust wishes and hops you are ill."

"That's nice of her."

"Royal Prance, I come to warn you of a lawful catastroscope. The Hounds of Gobbolot have landed."

"The Hounds of Gobbolot?"

"Wired creatures—" started Jeepio.

"I think you mean *weird*," said Willie.

"Wired creatures constricted by your Uncle Rumpus Pundar."

At the very mention of the name Willie remembered the pale, unhappy features of his Uncle Rumpus, the only one in the family with brains.

"What are these hounds like?" asked Willie.

"Big," said Jeepio. "Square luminous eyes, with hypnotic poors."

"Are they dangerous?" asked Willie.

"They are bent on ivel!" said Jeepio.

"Isn't that some kind of cheese?" asked Willie.

"By our concubations they landed a wok ago," said Jeepio, starting to fizz round his edges. "Probably not more than two kilogrammes from this very spit as the cow flees."

"Cows don't usually fly," said Willie. "Not round here."

"I bog you to soss your interraptions, Royal Prance," said Jeepio, blue sparks flashing round his feet as if someone had stuck sparklers between his toes and lit them. "It is noo tim for my transmotion." He started to judder like a cat in a cartoon. "Soon I must varnish. But never forgit the Hounds of Gobbolot. Bewitch them!"

"I think you mean *beware*," said Willie.

"And bewitch your Uncle Rumpus as will. And his drudded Perfectoscope."

"Drudded Perfectoscope?" said Willie. "What does it do?"

"Makes everyone peefect," said Jeepio.

12

"Peefect?" said Willie.

"I didn't say *peefect*," said Jeepio, "I said—"

But before he could finish he varnished through the coal-house roof in a sputter of sparks.

FOUR

The Hounds of Gobbolot

Shrimp Salmon was so upset as he started through the allotments that he didn't notice four luminous eyes watching him from the darkness ahead.

So Reggie thought he was too small to fight, did he! "Come back when you've grown up a bit, Shrimp," Reggie had said. And Knocker Bowles had shouted, "Or when you haven't just let in twenty-seven goals!"

It was true that this morning Shrimp had let in twenty-seven goals against Oldwistle Junior Mixed. It was a disgrace, really. Miss Minsky had come to watch but had gone just after he made this incredible dive to the right as the ball trickled in to his left.

The streetlights were behind him now and though his eyes were used to the darkness he still didn't see the two pairs of eyes coming towards him. What he did notice was the strange mist swirling round his feet.

Funny, he thought. Down at the quarry it had been a lovely clear night. He remembered looking up and seeing millions of stars. Now there was all this funny mist around him.

Then, just as he reached Mr Fletcher's allotment, the mist cleared and he saw two huge creatures padding towards him.

They were a bit like dogs, really, only much bigger. Mr Longstaff had a lurcher that was big. His name was Oscar but nobody ever called him that. Nobody ever called him anything. They just looked the other way. It was the same with the other dogs in Muckyford. For years Oscar had been prowling the streets looking for a fight but so far he hadn't had one. If another dog saw him it just went in early for its tea.

But these creatures were much bigger than Oscar.

"Good evening," said the first one,

leaning over Shrimp. "Permit us to introduce ourselves." He smiled as he spoke, but behind the smile Shrimp thought he saw something sharp and nasty. "We are the Hounds of Gobbolot. I am Cecil, and this is Claud. Might we possibly enquire your name?"

"Shrimp Salmon," said Shrimp.

"Shrimp? Thou art surely not a crustacean?"

"Pardon?" said Shrimp.

"You have not a segmented body and a hard external shell?"

"Not that I know of. It's me nickname."

"Ah! I see. What do you think, Claud?" the first Hound asked.

"He *is* rather small, Cecil."

"I agree. But he may still be an interesting specimen for our master. He could always be – improved."

"Quite so."

Cecil smiled again. This time Shrimp distinctly saw the glint of steel teeth.

"Don't worry, old chap," said Cecil.

"Just look into my eyes."

As the Hound came towards him its large blue eyes spun round in ever-decreasing circles until Shrimp's brain went as vacant as it usually did in Miss Minsky's tests.

"This won't hurt at all," said Cecil, smiling in a particularly nasty way. "Or hardly!"

Fair Bamboozled

Next morning, Sunday, Willie called at Shrimp's house on his way to the allotments with his tasty titbits.

But Shrimp's mam said he wasn't in.

"He has us fair bamboozled, Willie," she said. "He were up at six this morning learning his tables!"

"He brought us a cup of tea in bed and washed up," said his dad, looking dumbfounded. "And before that he vacuumed his rabbit hutch."

"Twice," said his mam. "He'll be most likely round at the rec."

"Thanks, Mrs Salmon," said Willie.

Reggie Flagg's gang were in the rec, making arrows out of bent bits of wood under the supervision of Knocker Bowles. They were clustered at the top end because Mr Longshank's lurcher was down at the bottom, smelling the daisies.

Nobody had set eyes on Shrimp.

"Most likely gone to practise his goal-keeping!" sniggered Knocker.

"Or Mr Longshank's lurcher has swallied him!" said Nogger Flobb.

When he said that, Mr Longstaff's lurcher looked towards him, almost as if he had suddenly been gifted with some sort of intelligence. Nogger went the colour of bluetop milk. But after a tick Oscar barged off through a gap in the fence, no doubt looking for a fight.

"Fancy joining my army now, Willie?" asked Reggie. "We're still a man short."

"No, thanks," Willie answered politely.

"He's scared!" said Knocker Bowles.

"I'm not," replied Willie as he turned away.

He didn't point out that all the arrows were made of bent wood and would obviously fly round in circles.

On Monday morning Willie was relieved to

see Shrimp waiting for him at the bottom of Clogg Street so they could walk to school together.

But straight away he noticed something wrong.

There was a terrible glazed look in Shrimp's eyes.

"You OK?" Willie asked him.

"Champion," said Shrimp, gazing dully ahead.

"What were you doing yesterday?"

"Picking up litter," said Shrimp. "Fifty-four bagfuls."

"What's up, Shrimp?"

"Opposite of down," said Shrimp. "Adverb from the Old English word *up*, *upp*, or *uppe*."

"Flipping heck!" said Willie.

"Nine times nineteen is one hundred and seventy-one," said Shrimp.

Must be the shock of the match, thought Willie. Nobody would feel too perky after letting in twenty-seven goals. Willie wanted to say something cheery to his little pal but what can you say to somebody who's just let in twenty-seven goals? Then he remembered that the match before Shrimp had let in forty-one goals so he said, "Still, better than last time."

"Forty-one minus twenty-seven is fourteen," said Shrimp smiling grimly, "and fourteen times nine is one hundred and twenty-six."

"What you doing all this for, Shrimp?"

"Tables test today."

"Miss Minsky's only goes up to twelve."

"Fifteen times nine is a hundred and thirty-five," said Shrimp.

Then Willie noticed something else unusual about his pal. As long as he could remember there had been a permanent tide-mark round his neck. Now it was gone. Together with the wax in his lugholes.

"You sure you're all right?" asked Willie. No sooner were the words out of his mouth than Shrimp turned right and stepped off the pavement under the wheels of a bus that was twenty minutes late.

Willie only just pulled him back in time.

"Ecky thump!" said Willie. "You were nearly a gonner then!"

" 'We are such stuff as dreams are made on'," said Shrimp, " 'and our little life is rounded with a sleep'."

"Yer what, Shrimp?"

"Shakespeare," explained Shrimp. "*The Tempest*. Act 1V, scene 1."

Willie realised then how bad things were. When folks started spouting Shakespeare things *had* to be serious. He fell into step with his pal and didn't speak again until they went through the school gates. Then he saw something worse.

Sally Mow was talking to Nathan Peabody again – this time about somebody called Paddy Rewsky who probably played for Northern Ireland.

"Fancy a game of footer, Willie?" asked Shrimp. "Sixteen times nine is one hundred and forty-four, same as twelve times twelve and twenty-four times six."

Shrimp took his stance against the bike-shed wall and crouched forward. When he played goalie he put his whole heart and soul into it, dived this way and that without a thought for his safety; it was just a pity he always dived the wrong way.

Willie balanced the ball on a crisp packet and prepared to take his first shot. His secret dream was one day to wear the famous Muckyford United strip, the one with Krogenpop Lager scrawled all over it in blobby writing. His idol was Vivien Clogend, the Muckyford striker. But although he had forty-one pictures of him in almost every conceivable position known to man it had never done Willie any good. His feet seemed to be the wrong shape for kicking footballs. He aimed for the top-left corner but the ball spiralled off his toe, bounced off the baldy napper of Mr Miley, the headmaster – who only smiled because he was a decent sort – and shot like a rocket for the bottom right corner of the bike-shed wall.

And it was then that Willie got the biggest shock of all.

Because Shrimp Salmon dived the right way and made a save!

SIX

Fight!

It was the same in the classroom.

Shrimp came top in the tables test for the first time, even beating Nathan Peabody, who went the colour of a poorly cucumber when he heard the result.

Miss Minsky was flabgustipated.

"However did you manage that?" she asked Shrimp.

"Ninety-eight times nine is eight hundred and eighty-two, miss," Shrimp replied.

"Don't overdo things," she advised. "You could strain your brain."

After that she started telling them about the First World War. She told them about Emmeline Pankhurst who had chucked a brick through a window so that women could have the vote. Then she showed them a picture of Lord Kitchener who had a moustache like an overgrown privet hedge.

"Lord Kitchener wanted all the men to

volunteer for war," she said, "but some of them wouldn't. Many of them received white feathers from their lady-friends, as a sign that they were cowards."

"Men aren't cowards, miss," said Reggie Flagg, going red.

"Some are, Reginald. Have you forgotten how even the Roman legions needed a standard-bearer at the front to lead them into their battles? And they were very brave indeed. Not like the sort of man we have around today!" She glanced vaguely in the direction of Mr Watkins' classroom as she spoke. "Now, take out your topic books and write down your views on the First World War."

Shrimp wrote page after page – all perfect stuff.

Willie copied down the title, "The First World War", did some nice twirly bits round the edges, then drew a white knight clonking a black knight on the napper with one of those spiky things on the end of a long chain with a bubble coming out of his mouth saying, "Have at you, cur!"

The whole school team was shooting-in at Shrimp during playtime but nobody could score a goal past him: every time he dived the right way.

That wasn't the only thing worrying Willie.

The school disco was on Thursday and he still hadn't plucked up enough courage to ask Sally to go with him.

As it happened she was quite near him, listening to Nathan Peabody talk about somebody called Johann Sebastian Bach, so Willie – just trying to be friendly – said, "He plays for Denmark, doesn't he?"

"Pshaw!" said Nathan.

"You daft ha'porth," said Sally. "Johann Sebastian Bach doesn't play for nobody. He's been dead for donkey's years."

"Don't you know nothing, Scrimshaw?" said Nathan. "Johann Sebastian Bach wrote

'The Flight of the Bumblebee'. I thought everybody knew that!"

And they wandered away before Willie could think up a witty reply.

He felt sad as he watched them go. He wished he was brainy and could play a musical instrument. A kazoo would have done. To be honest, he'd never even heard of 'The Bite of the Flumblebee'.

"You still sure you don't want to join Reggie's army?" said a voice in his left ear.

Knocker Bowles was looking down at him.

"No, thanks," said Willie.

"OK!" said Knocker, and he knocked him down.

Before Willie had struggled to his feet a crowd had gathered round them shouting, "FIGHT! FIGHT! FIGHT!"

"Ready to join now, tha' weed?" said Knocker.

"No," said Willie.

So Knocker punched him on the nose and knocked him down again.

Willie really didn't want to fight. On the other hand, he couldn't allow Knocker Bowles to keep knocking him down all playtime. He had just made up his mind to knock Knocker Bowles into the middle of next Friday when a hand reached down to help him up.

It was Reggie Flagg.

"Lay off him, Knocker," he said. "Willie's not scared to fight. He's not scared of nowt. He's not even scared of Mr Longshank's lurcher. I bet he wouldn't even have been scared of them dogs we saw last night down at the quarry."

"What dogs?" asked Willie, wiping the blood off his nose with a bit of mucky rag.

"Ginormous," said Nogger Flobb. "Right funny eyes."

"Luminous, were they?" asked Willie.

"How did you know that?"

"What did they do?" asked Willie.

"We didn't hang around to find out," said Reggie. "It was hard to see because

29

of this mist all round them. Far as we could make out they were heading for the old abandoned tunnel entrance in the quarry face."

Willie knew it well. When they'd been kids they'd often gone in there for a dare. But nobody had ever got very far because of the dark.

"And summat else, Willie," said Nogger Flobb. "They were carrying something between them. It looked like a human body, like. A small one. About the size of—"

"About the size of Shrimp Salmon?" said Willie, turning to look in the direction of his little pal as he saved yet another shot.

"Aye! How did you know that, Willie?"

"Just a lucky guess," said Willie.

SEVEN

Signals for Help

After tea Willie popped upstairs to his bedroom and inspected his Superkid suit. He had a feeling he might be needing it soon.

If you'd seen it you might have thought it was an old plastic beach-ball. But Willie had only to slip it on and all his muscles expanded to their proper size and he could fly through the air and punch holes in brick walls. And when he pulled on his snazzy boots and donned the mask that concealed his identity (though not his nose – it would have taken a tent to cover his nose), he looked a right bobby-dazzler.

When he was sure his suit was OK he went downstairs and collected the apple peelings his mam had saved him for Samantha and Perce.

On his way to the allotments he called in at Shrimp's, but as he'd expected, Shrimp wasn't in.

"You don't know where he's gone, Mrs Salmon?" asked Willie.

"He reckoned he were going to cut all the old folks' hedges."

"We're right worried, Willie," said Mr Salmon, who was reading the *Muckyford Daily Lyre*. The front page headline read: ALLOTMENTS FOR CHOP.

"Is he still acting funny?" asked Willie.

"He were polishing me slippers tonight,"

said Mr Salmon sadly.

"And before that he shampooed the cat," said poor Mrs Salmon.

When Willie passed the old folks' homes he saw Shrimp cutting all their hedges, his clipper blades glinting in the evening sun.

"Fancy coming down the allotments?" Willie asked him.

"No, thanks," said Shrimp. "After I've cut all the hedges I'm going to mow all the lawns and then fill up all the coal buckets."

Old Mr Oldcastle came up to Willie as he was leaving.

"Can't you get him to give over, Willie?" he said.

"How do you mean, Mr Oldcastle?"

"If he keeps on doing all these jobs for us we'll soon have nowt left to keep our minds active. We'll all end up on the funny farm!"

"I'm sorry," said Willie as he went. "There's nothing I can do, just at present, Mr Oldcastle."

The whole world seemed gloomy. It wasn't just because his best pal was acting odd and Sally didn't like him. If the headline in the *Muckyford Daily Lyre* was right the allotments were to be sold to a millionaire building firm. And that would mean the end of Samantha and Perce because Mr Fletcher would not be able to afford anywhere else for them to live.

A lot of folks had campaigned for a long time to get rid of the allotments. They said they were smelly. But so far Councillor

Allgob had always put his foot down with a firm hand. NOBODY PUTS FINGER ON ALLOTMENTS OVER ALLGOB'S DEAD BODY, had been the headline last week.

Now it looked like he had changed his mind.

In a way, Willie could understand why. The Fairholme Development Company had offered to pay a load of money. And that was exactly what Muckyford was short of.

On the other hand, money wasn't everything.

The allotments might be smelly but they were home to a lot of happy hens and ducks and pigeons. Any night of the week you could see folks happily yanking up weeds or sitting in their cronky old chairs watching their onions grow or listening to blackbirds singing.

That had to be worth something.

As usual, Samantha and Perce were waiting by the gate when Willie got to Mr Fletcher's allotment. Perce seemed excited, running this way and that, grunting all the time, almost as if he was trying to tell Willie something. Samantha was on a long rope that was tied to a stake because she'd always fancied her chances in the Grand National. Twice she had leapt over the allotment fence and got down on to the road.

She looked sad. But then she always did. Even her name had a sad story attached to it. During the war, Mr Fletcher had fallen in love with an evacuee called Samantha, but when she had been returned to her home in Liverpuddle he had lost contact with her. He still loved her after all those years, still thought of her every day.

"How do, you two," Willie said. "Been a champion day."

Perce grunted his agreement and Samantha hung her head even lower. Willie always talked to animals though he couldn't understand their replies – unless he had his magic suit on.

"Weather forecast's bad," he told them as he gave them the apple peelings. "A cold front's drifting down from Iceland."

Samantha coughed.

"And my pal Shrimp's acting right funny as well," he said.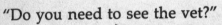

At once Perce got up on his hind legs and crossed his front legs this way and that.

"What's up, Perce?" he asked. "Do you need to see the vet?"

Perce shook his head and started crossing and uncrossing even more.

Then Willie realised what was happening. Perce was using a method of signalling called semaphore. Willie had read all about it in his *Monster Boy's Book of Facts*. Sailors used flags to send messages by semaphore.

"You're trying to tell me something, aren't you, Perce?"

Perce nodded and crossed his legs again.

"Three letters?" said Willie. "First letter? Second letter? Then first letter again?

Right. I'll look it
up when I get back."
At that moment
they all heard
a cry for help
and Perce
dropped down
on all fours and
galloped over to
the side of the

allotment that overlooked the quarry. He
looked back at Willie and squealed.

Willie hurried over and looked down into
the quarry.

It was hard to
be sure what he
saw because of
the swirling mist.
But it looked
like two huge
dogs heading for
the tunnel
entrance.

They seemed to have luminous eyes.

Between them they were carrying a fat old feller with a baldy napper who looked very like Willie's headmaster.

EIGHT

Grey Feathers

The next morning all the girls started giving grey feathers to boys who hadn't joined Reggie Flagg's army. They would have given white ones only they couldn't find any in Muckyford.

When Willie looked round at Sally he saw with relief that she wasn't holding out any grey feathers towards him. But she was talking to Nathan Peabody again, this time about somebody called Rip Yerkorsetsoff.

"Excuse me butting in," Willie said, "but could I have a word?"

"You've had ten already!" said Nathan, who was brilliant at sums.

"What is it, Willie?" Sally asked.

"There's summat right serious going on, Sally," said Willie.

"You mean about this daft gang Reggie Flagg's getting up?"

"Pshaw!" said Nathan Peabody.

"Nathan is a conscientious inspector, Willie," she explained.

"What's that mean?"

"It means he doesn't believe in fighting."

"On principle!" added Nathan.

"It's nowt to do with Reggie Flagg, Sal," said Willie. "It's just that after I'd fed Samantha and Perce last night I looked down into the limestone quarry and saw something."

"What was it?" asked Nathan scoffily. "Limestone?"

"No," said Willie. "I saw them big dogs everybody's talking about."

"I suppose they had luminous eyes!" sneered Nathan.

"They had, as a matter of fact."

"And mist swirling round them?"

"Aye."

"Pshaw!" said Nathan.

"You don't believe all that stuff, Willie?" said Sal. "Reggie's just saying that to keep folks out of the quarry. He

42

thinks he owns it."

"But I saw them, Sal, and they were carrying somebody. I'd like to see the headmaster about this straight away – if somebody would come with me, like."

"I might point out, Scrimshaw, that Mr Miley will be very busy this morning," said Nathan. "Councillor Allgob and his good lady wife are coming specially to hear me play my trumpet."

"Come on then, you daft lummock," said Sal. "I'll come with you."

They could hardly get into the school secretary's office because half the staff were already in there. The secretary's specs were steamed up and at first she wouldn't let them in to see Mr Miley.

"Mr Watkins is with him at the moment, Willie," she said, "making final changes to the new curriculum Mr Miley thought up last night."

Her lip wobbled as she spoke. Glancing

round, Willie saw that all her nice posters of fluffy kittens and baby elephants had been taken down to make room for a plan of the new curriculum.

It was a multi-coloured affair stretching over all the walls. The title was, "An Easy-to-Read Explanation of My New Timetable", but most of the teachers looked shell-shocked.

Mrs Plumbody was scrabbling through her handbag, muttering "Smelly salts! Smelly salts!" Mr Burke was smoking his pipe upside-down. As far as Willie could see the new timetable allowed everybody to be anywhere except where they were supposed to be in the first place. Except on Fridays, that is, when Willie wasn't sure about anything.

When Willie and Sal were finally allowed in to see the headmaster he had his back to them. He was jabbing pins in something called, "Minor Changes to the Miley Method of the Infinitely Adaptable Timetable". It wasn't as big as the one in the secretary's office – this one was only two and a half walls long. But Willie could see it was growing.

"Shouldn't we wait till next year before we use your new timetable, Mr Miley?" Mr Watkins was saying. "I mean, after your Early Retirement?"

"Early Retirement?" said Mr Miley, laughing mirthlessly. "No time for that now! My perfect new timetable is about to shake the world!"

"I can believe that, Headmaster," said Mr Watkins. He turned away to wipe his brow and Willie saw that his face was as grey and soggy as an old shower-mat. "Hello, you two," he said. "What do you want?"

"We'd like to see the headmaster, sir," said Willie, "if that's OK. About something right important."

"*Very*," corrected Mr Watkins, who was keen on grammar.

"*Very* right important, sir," said Willie, who was keen to please.

"What is it, Scrimshaw W?" asked Mr Miley as he swung round.

Willie had never been called that before and for a moment he wondered if the headmaster meant somebody else. Then Willie saw the glazed look in Mr Miley's eyes and he guessed the reason for his strange behaviour. He'd seen that glazed look before. In Shrimp Salmon's eyes.

"It doesn't matter, sir," he said. "I'm sorry for wasting your time."

NINE

Dangerous Doings

Sally wasn't too impressed when Willie explained about the glazed eyes.

"But *your* eyes are always glazed over, Willie," she said.

"I know, Sal, but with me it's natural. I'm sure these big dogs down the quarry are hypnotising folk and then somehow changing them."

"You're crackers, Willie," she said.

She was more impressed when Councillor Allgob arrived.

Councillor Allgob normally wore a flat hat and a shabby old raincoat. This time he clanked into the hall wearing his mayoral chains over a new suit and a posh pair of boots from the Co-op. Usually he bored everybody silly with long speeches but this time he said, "My dear constituent parts, it is my honour to welcome you to this performance by an outstanding young virtuoso on the trumpet," and sat down.

Everybody looked flabgustipated and Sally turned round and said, "You were right, Willie! There *is* something funny going on."

Nathan played very well – making only three or four fluffs as far as Willie could make out – but Willie was more interested in what Sally had just said and the way she had smiled at him.

He wondered if he was in with a chance now.

He still wasn't too sure, though. He wished he was a virtuoso on something.

The fact was, he wasn't good at anything, not even conkers.

Worst of all, he didn't have any principles, not like Nathan Peabody. To be honest, he wasn't right sure what principles were. But he'd have to see about getting a few as soon as he could.

When he got home he asked his mam what principles were, but she said she was too busy baking rock cakes to answer daft questions. His dad suspected they were summat foreign. His sister said it was the name of a shop, which was barmy.

He was just forcing down his fourth slice of jam and bread when there was a knock at their back door and his mam shouted from the kitchen, "Young lady to see you, Our Willie!"

And Sally Mow came in their house.

"Look at Our Willie!" said Darleen. "Red in the face and pink all over! When you two getting wed?"

"Nobody round here good enough," said

Sally, joking. "Anyroad, me mam sez I've to stick in at school and get a load of ologies so I can get a good job."

"What you going to be?" asked Darleen.

"I might be an astronaut," said Sally. "There's nowt round here. There's bound to be more going on in space. Or I might be a parachutist. I like jumping off the quarry top."

"You want to mind what you're doing down there," said Willie's dad. "There's been some nasty rumours flying round."

"I know," said Sally. "That's why we're going down to investigate. Aren't we, Willie?"

"If you like," said Willie, pretending he wasn't worried either way. "But first I have to call in at Mr Fletcher's allotment."

Before they went out Willie nipped upstairs and changed into his magic suit, then put his ordinary clothes back on top and hid his mask in his pocket. As soon as he put on the suit he nearly bobbed up to the ceiling, so when he picked up the titbits from the kitchen he shoved a couple of his mam's rock cakes in his pockets to weigh him down.

Stomper, Sally's dog, was waiting for them in the yard. Sally hadn't brought him in the house because he had the sort of tail that knocks vases over. He strutted ahead of them down Balmoral Crescent until they saw Mr Longstaff's lurcher. Then Sally had to pick him up and carry him, he was that scared.

In the rec Reggie Flagg and his army were trying to hit a target with their bendy arrows but all of them were going round in circles.

"We're still short of a man, Willie," said Reggie. "We're going to dig our trenches on the hill down the tip tonight. What about it?"

"No thanks."

"Are you a man – or a mouse, Scrimshaw?" asked Knocker Bowles.

Willie pretended he hadn't heard.

"I'll join your army if you like, Reggie," said Sally.

"Don't be soft!" said Knocker Bowles. "Girls can't fight!"

"Can't they?" said Sally. "I'll fight you any day of the week!"

All the way through the allotments Willie was scared Sally would hand him a grey feather or something because he hadn't volunteered for Reggie's army. But she didn't.

As he was feeding Samantha and Perce their titbits he said, "I worked out your message, Perce. You were signalling SOS, weren't you? How can I help?"

"It's a waste of time talking to animals, you know," Sally told him.

Willie said nothing.

"A feller with a face as long as a fiddle keeps flying up and down the air-shaft on the tip," said Perce. Willie smiled. That was

Uncle Rumpus, all right. "He has two huge dogs which we saw kidnapping your pal Shrimp Salmon on Saturday night. I think he's also captured the mayor and your headmaster."

"I think you're right, Perce," said Willie.

"You know what, Willie Scrimshaw?" said Sally as they came away. "You must be entirely nuts and bananas!"

"I just can't help it, Sal!" he said.

Willie and Sally were halfway across the quarry floor when strange mist began to swirl round them. (It reminded Willie of the stuff they used at Muckyford Alhambra when his Aunty Flora took him to the pantomime.) Then out of the mist came the two ginormous Hounds, their eyes blazing.

"What in heck are they?" asked Sally.

"I'll tell you something," said Stomper. "They sure ain't dogs!"

(Sally didn't hear these words, of course, but Willie did.)

"How do you know, Stomper?" he asked.

"No niff," said Stomper.

"You talking to animals again?" said Sally.

The Hounds were very close now. They opened their huge jaws and growled. Willie had never seen such huge teeth. They didn't look real, somehow. More like his dad's, only bigger.

"You think we'd better do a bunk, Sal?" asked Willie.

"Not on your nelly!" said Sal. "Stomper will protect us."

"I don't think so, Sal," said Willie.

He'd heard a scuttering of stones behind him, and turning round he saw Stomper heading out of the quarry entrance at ninety miles an hour.

TEN

Rock Cakes

Willie wasn't worried about himself, of course.

But he *was* worried about Sally.

The Hounds of Gobbolot were near now. Their eyes became bigger and bluer and began to twirl round. Willie couldn't help noticing their teeth were like those long needles dentists shove in your gums.

"You think we'd better go, Sal?" said Willie.

"I'm not scared of dogs!"

"Maybe they're not dogs," said Willie, who had a feeling that Stomper had been right. When Sally wasn't watching he took off his jam-jar specs and switched on his X-ray eyes. Between the Hounds' ears there was nothing but a mass of wires and transistors. It was like looking at the inside of his remote control Kopcar.

Beside him he heard Sally say something

but her voice trailed off sleepily. When Willie looked at her he saw that her eyes were closed and that she was breathing deeply.

"Your female looks a jolly interesting specimen, Cecil," said the Hound opposite Willie.

"Most interesting, Claud. Rumpus Pundar will be delighted that we have found two more creatures for his Perfectoscope."

"Are you in control of her mind now?"

"Yes, though she did put up strong resistance, rather like the young female teacher we delivered to our master earlier. How are you doing with the boy creature, Claud?"

"I seem to be encountering slight opposition."

That was putting it mildly. Willie was fighting with every fibre of his superhuman powers to stay awake. In the past few seconds the pale, unhappy features of Uncle Rumpus seemed to have loomed up in his head. *I am extremely brainy and therefore know what is best for you,* his uncle's voice kept saying. *Sleep now. Let me take charge.*

Willie struggled hard against the voice but with every second that passed his willpower weakened. At the same time the Hound called Cecil had taken hold of Sally's bomber jacket and was dragging her away in his jaws.

Willie gritted his teeth and took a step forward.

"I order you to leave that girl alone!" he said.

Cecil looked amused.

"I warn you to let go of that girl."

"Can't do that, old man. Orders are orders."

"For the third and final time," said Willie.

Cecil laughed.

"Very well!" said Willie.

He delivered a punch that would have gone through a brick wall. It had no effect on Cecil. Willie delivered another of his thunderbolts. Cecil simply smiled. Willie realised that his strength was useless against these robots. No weapon on earth could stop them. Or was there one weapon that could?

He took one of his mam's rock cakes from his pocket and flung it hard. It bounced off Cecil's snoot and made his eyes slide sideways. The second rock cake made his jaws sag open. As Sally slipped to the ground Willie scooped her up and whooshed her high into the air.

Up and up he went. Below him he saw Stomper scuttling for home through the allotments and Samantha and Perce gazing up in amazement. He saw all of Muckyford below him: the shut-down mills, the world-famous gasworks and Goodiland, the biggest shoppers' paradise in the North.

Willie headed for the top of the hill above the tip, hardly noticing Reggie Flagg and his army digging their trenches. He laid Sal down gently on a bunch of springy grass. He put on his mask, then took off his ordinary clothes and stuffed them in a pocket of his magic suit. When his disguise was complete he called softly:

"Awake, o Earth maiden!"

"What the flip's going on?" asked Sally, sitting up. When she saw Willie she said, "Oh, it's you again!" for this was not the first time Superkid had rescued her.

"Where's that lummock, Willie Scrimshaw?"

"Fear not," said Willie. "I have returned him safely to his home."

"Why do you always talk funny? Can't you talk proper English?"

Willie was trying to think up an answer to that one when behind him he heard Reggie and his army scrambling up the slope.

"Hail and farewell, Earth maiden!" said Willie and with a flash of sparks he vanished into the blue up yonder.

"What's going on, Sally?" asked Reggie Flagg when he reached her.

"What do you mean?"

"We've just seen Willie Scrimshaw flying over the tip, all long and skinny with a nose sticking out like I don't know what!"

"Have you cloth between your ears, or what, Reggie Flagg?" said Sally. "Willie Scrimshaw can't fly."

"You're right, Sal," said Reggie. "It must've been Concorde!"

ELEVEN

Further Flabgustipation

Shrimp said a funny thing as they walked to school next morning.

As usual, a queue of folks was waiting at the Cemetery Road bus stop, red-faced and angry because the bus was late.

But this time the folks were hopping mad.

"I'll masecrate that driver when he comes!" said a woman who looked fit to explode.

"I'll give you a hand," said the man next to her.

"What's the time, Shrimp?" asked Willie.

Shrimp's watch was one of those right useful ones that played "God Save the Queen" backwards in the middle of assemblies and could tell you when the next flood was due in Timbuctoo. It was such a good watch it took him two minutes to work out the time.

"Eight thirty-two," he said.

"Flipping heck!" said Willie. "That means the bus from Tintwistle is twenty minutes late!"

"Late?" said Shrimp as they crossed the road. "But why don't the buses run on time? Aren't they supposed to?"

Willie was flabgustipated. Muckyford buses *always* ran late. He and Shrimp had been passing that bus stop for donkey's years and not once had they seen a bus arrive on time. But he didn't say anything. He had a feeling there was no getting past those glazed eyes.

In any case Shrimp was muttering something.

"What you say, Shrimp?"

"Spelling test this morning," he said. "V-A-C-U-O-U-S."

"What's that word?"

"Vacuous," said Shrimp.

"What's it mean?"

"Haven't a clue, but I know how to spell it!"

Willie felt sad. Not because he was jealous. Willie was hopeless at spelling, always had been. But he *did* think your heart had to be in a thing for it to mean anything. And how could your heart be in vacu-whatever-it-was if you hadn't a clue what it meant?

It was the same when they got in the school yard. Shrimp dived this way and that making brilliant saves but all the time looking as if he'd just as soon be dusting his mam's front-room ornaments.

And it was worse still when they went in the classroom. Miss Minsky usually wore trousers and looked dead strict. This morning she was wearing a flowery dress and a load of pongy scent. She even had a rose stuck in her hair. "Good morning, boys and girls," she said.

She'd never said that before. (She always put the girls first.) And her eyes – which usually glittered like knives – had the same dull look as Shrimp's and the headmaster's.

All that day she was the perfect teacher. In the history lesson she didn't once mention Emily Pancake and her votes for women, or Lord Fitted Kitchen and his flipping white feathers for men. In the spelling test she gave them useful words like *conkers* and *centre-forward* – the sort that were always cropping up in conversations.

She even seemed to get the hang of Mr Miley's "Infinitely Adaptable Timetable" so that after dinner everybody was allowed to do their own thing. Charlie Woodhead chased Emily Brew round and round the room (he had this thing about her). The noisy boys formed a pop group called The Raving Loonies, the quiet ones whanged clay balls across the room. Most of the girls formed discussion groups to discuss their charm bracelets. The noise was deafening. When Mr Miley came in he smiled gravely and said, "Jolly good, carry on," and went out.

Willie worked on his nineteenth project on Knights in Dayes of Olde, but it was hard to concentrate. It wasn't just the noise. Why was Miss Minsky all of a sudden ponging of scent and roses? What was his Uncle Rumpus up to with his drudded Perfecto-scope? What *was* a drudded Perfectoscope anyroad? He supposed that after tea he'd just have to put on his magic suit and find out.

Just as Willie was drawing a good knight

attacking a bad knight with a lance that looked very like his mam's new clothes prop, Mr Watkins came in and shouted above the din, "Everything all right, Miss Minsky?"

"Fine," she said. "How kind of you to ask, Mr Watkins."

And she smiled at him.

There was a rush of blood to poor Mr Watkins' head and his jaw dropped open like a steam shovel.

"You wouldn't by any chance like a lift home this evening, Miss Minsky?" he asked.

"I would indeed," said Miss Minsky.

"I say!" said Mr Watkins. "I mean to say, I say!"

TWELVE

Events at Sheep's Bottom Clough

Mr Watkins could hardly believe his luck.

And his luck got better.

As he drove Miss Minsky home, the sun came out to lend a romantic glow to Muckyford. When he suggested they should go for a ramble after tea she agreed at once.

Ever since he had first seen her blow her whistle during a netball practice, Mr Watkins had been in love with Miss Minsky, and especially with the fiery sparkles in her eyes.

He had tried everything to win her approval. He had invited her to a talk at Muckyford Museum on the contents of mummies' tummies, but unfortunately she had to wash her hair. On Guy Fawkes' night he had bought her a toffee apple and she had told him to drop it in the litter-bin because they rotted the teeth. And at last year's Fun For All Christmas

Disco he had asked her to do the Birdy Song with him but she had told him – her eyes especially sparkling – that the time was past when men should invite women on to the dance floor. Now, she had said, it was the turn of the women to ask. All night he had sat surrounded by children bouncing up and down like demented kangaroos, hoping that she would ask him to dance; but she never had.

Now, he thought, things had changed.

After tea he brushed his teeth twice, cut off some whiskers that were poking down his nose and splashed on lashings of Apeman (hoping it would have half the effect promised in the TV advert).

When he called at her lodgings she was already waiting. As he opened the car door for her she smiled so much he almost fell off the pavement.

He drove her to the local beauty spot, Sheep's Bottom Clough. The valley was bathed in golden light as they strolled through the fields surrounded by the plaintive baa-ings of sheep. The midges – a pest in these parts – buzzed off at the first whiff of Apeman. As he helped her over a stile their hands met and, after that, never came unstuck.

How small her hand is, he thought. How cold. *Cold hand, warm heart*, was a saying he had often heard his dear mother utter. Judging by the smile on Miss Minsky's face, his dear mother must have been right.

When they stopped for a moment by a gargling brook he could restrain his passion no longer. *It's now or never, Rodney!* he thought.

He bent down and kissed her softly on the cheek.

Miss Minsky did not step back. (If anything, she lunged forward.)

"You don't mind, Miss Minsky?" he said.

"Why should I, Mr Watkins?"

"Please call me Rodney," he said.

"Rodney!" she repeated, quite overcome. "What a lovely name!"

If ever there was a time for proposing marriage, it had to be now. Mr Watkins leaned forward to utter the magic words.

But the words never came.

This close to Miss Minsky he realised at last the terrible truth. The fiery sparkles had gone from her eyes. They were blurred, almost as if she were peering through spectacles the thickness of Scrimshaw's.

He should have known from the smile, of course, from that very first moment in the classroom.

The girl he held in his arms was not the real Miss Minsky!

THIRTEEN

A Right Funny Carry-on

High above Mr Watkins, at this tragic moment, floated Willie Scrimshaw, a tear dimming his eye as he watched the scene beneath him.

On his way home from school he had seen how bad things were. As he and Shrimp passed the Cemetery Road bus stop Willie noticed that none of the people at the bus stop were moaning about late buses. All of them were staring straight ahead and looking bored.

At first Willie didn't understand. Then he saw the 3.50 from Tintwistle heaving into view, a glassy-eyed driver at the wheel. "Afternoon, folks," he said, smiling as he hissed the door open.

Muckyford bus drivers didn't usually say things like that. And never in his life had Willie seen one smile.

"What's the time, Shrimp?" he asked, and

after two minutes Shrimp replied, "Three-fifty exactly."

"Flipping heck!"

"What's up?"

"The buses are running on time!"

Willie realised what a catastroscope that could be. If *all* the buses ran on time nobody would have anything to complain about. The citizens of Muckyford would have been deprived of their favourite pastime. It would be almost as bad as shutting all the chip shops.

Something had to be done soon about Uncle Rumpus and his drudded Perfecto-scope. And soon.

Willie was even more worried when he went home for his tea.

His dad was in the kitchen wearing a pinny and studying a book called *Delia Cobblestone's Mediterranean Cookery*. Willie had never seen his dad in a pinny before, let alone reading a book; as a matter of fact, he'd never seen him in the kitchen before, except when he was passing through on his way to the Club.

"You all right, Dad?" he asked.

"Champion, lad." His dad's eyes were glazed over like Shrimp's and all the rest. "Just made your mam a nice cup of tea and now I'm making supper. New French recipe."

In the other room Willie heard his mam burst into tears.

"Your pocket money's on the table, lad," his dad said, smiling (a thing he never did at pocket-money time). "I've put it up to five quid."

"What's going on, Mam?" asked Willie when he went in the other room.

"Don't ask me, Willie," his mam said, crying into her tea. "Your dad's been acting funny since he came back from the bookies."

"Did he go round by the quarry?"

"He would do."

"I see," said Willie.

"Whatever are we going to do?" his mam said, crying again in her teacup. "He won't smoke his pipe or nothing. All he wants to do is cook and wash up!"

And a few minutes later Darleen burst through the door in tears. "Listen to this!" she said. "Wayne's stopped drinking Kangaroo Lager!"

That was a shock to them all: even Mr Scrimshaw paused as he chopped up garlic. Kangaroo Lager was advertised as the lager with the kick of the Outback. Wayne had always sworn by it (and Wayne swore quite a lot).

"*And* he's had the tints taken out of his hair!" Darleen screamed before she rushed up to her room.

"My Gawd!" said Mrs Scrimshaw, collapsing back into Dad's chair. "What's the world coming to!"

Willie knew then how desperate things were. He had an extra slice of jam and bread, then went up to his room and changed into his magic suit.

All the time his poor sister sobbed in the next room; only a week ago Willie had heard her and Wayne giggling as they practised the tango or touched up the tints in his hair.

"Not long now, Darleen," he muttered to himself.

In the mirror of his wardrobe he watched his muscles expand. He took two practice whizzes round the ceiling, almost dragging his *Rainforests of the World* map off the wall

as he passed it, so powerful was his jet-
stream. Then he put the remote control unit
from his Kopcar in one of his zip pockets,
pulled his mask down over as much of his
nose as possible, then climbed out on to his
windowsill.

"Not a-flipping-gain!" said next-door's cat on the back-yard wall.

Willie smiled as he looked towards the Allgob Memorial Hospital where he had first appeared on this earth, causing something of a stir because his mam had just gone in with a bad case of suspected wind. Not only that, he was the first child to be born already wearing a pair of specs (placed there to hide the power of his X-ray eyes, of course).

Looking up, he could see the stars twinkling in the infinite spaces of space. He wondered how his other mam and dad were getting on. He liked his Earth mam and dad. They were all right, really – though Willie was worried about his dad giving him five quid pocket money: that didn't seem right, somehow. But it was strange to think his name was not really Willie Scrimshaw, but Prince Dingbat Bogholler; that his dad was an Obsblud of the First Order and his mam nothing less than an Inglenuke! What a funny old world it was!

Then he took off in a blaze of sparks that left next-door's cat gasping for breath.

Indeed, so spectacular was Willie's take-off that he failed to notice Sally Mow knocking at the back door.

"What do you want, lass?" asked Mr Scrimshaw, who was also crying now (but only because he was chopping up onions).

"Your Willie coming out to play?"

"He's up in his bedroom," said Mr Scrimshaw. "I'll fetch him if you like." He went off to look, but of course he couldn't find Willie. "His mother thinks he might have gone down the quarry," he said cheerily when he came back. "Why don't you go down there to look?"

"I will do, Mr Scrimshaw," she said.

"If you see him, tell him he forgot the scraps for Samantha and Perce," said Mr Scrimshaw. "First time he's done that."

"OK, Mr Scrimshaw," said Sally.

Then off she went to the quarry.

And I'm sure you can imagine what happened.

FOURTEEN

Cod Lumps

Meanwhile, Willie was flying over the tip. When he was directly over the pit-shaft he dived straight down it.

At the bottom a tunnel led towards the quarry. A mile along it Willie came to a steel wall which even his X-ray eyes could not see through. He tried to move it with his superhuman power, but couldn't.

He was just beginning to think he was beaten when the steel wall slid upwards and Willie saw a chap with a face like a disappointed dachshund.

"Come in, dear nephew. What kept you so long?"

Uncle Rumpus was standing by a kind of glass coffin. Just behind him, chained to the wall, the Hounds of Gobbolot smiled their menace.

"What are you up to, Uncle?" asked Willie.

"Haven't you worked that out yet?"

"Whatever it is, your game is up," said Willie.

"No game, dear boy. This is for real. Your dear demented father would never listen to me so I had to come here to make my perfect world."

"Perfect world? Where are all the people that your dastardly Hounds have carried off?"

"Here's the latest specimen, if you're interested," said Rumpus, "in my Perfecto-scope."

"So that's your drudded Perfectoscope!" said Willie.

"*Dreaded*," corrected his Uncle Rumpus. "There's no such word as *drudded*. You never were very bright."

He opened the lid of the glass cabinet and Willie saw Sally Mow lying quite still, her face slightly frosted, her lips turning blue. But she wasn't dead. Even as Willie watched she opened one eye and said in a sleepy voice: "Oh, there you are, Superkid. About time. This feller's trying to make me perfect! He must be crackers."

"Cheeky child!" said Uncle Rumpus, closing the lid on her.

Willie was about to spring forward but Rumpus held up a warning hand. "Have a care, Royal Prince. To stop the process now could be dangerous. By the way, here are your other friends." He gestured behind him and Willie saw rack after rack filled with Muckyford folk, all lying as stiff as frozen cod-lumps.

"Murderer!" said Willie, gnashing his near-perfect teeth.

"Not at all, dear boy! Deep freeze, nothing more. One or two might feel a slight chill in their toes – and so forth – but that is all. None of them will die. All are in a state of suspended animation. Science is so wonderful, don't you think?"

"But what is it all for, Uncle Rumpus?"

"I am making a perfect world, dear boy. A world where everyone will be happy."

"Happy? People all over Muckyford are standing at bus stops looking bored because the buses are running on time. That means they've got nothing to complain about any more. You've made them *un*happy, Uncle Rumpus."

"People always complain when you're making things perfect for them. But they'll soon get the hang of it in a hundred years or so."

"Won't they be slightly dead by then?"

"Not at all, dear boy. In theory, my perfect

people should go on running forever. A few new transistors now and then, a drop of oil here and there. In a thousand years I shall have rearranged the world for them. No more messy rainforests. No muddy paths or bendy roads."

"But why?"

"Must have straight roads, dear boy.

Don't you see? Fewer accidents. Less petrol used. Eventually, of course, you won't even have to drive at all. Just get in your car and tell it where to go."

"But there'll be no fun in that!" said Willie.

"You don't understand, my dear boy. People might not enjoy it now but when they're perfect they will."

"You really think you can make perfect people?"

"I *know* I can. When this female specimen here is frozen stiff all I have to do is replace her with a lump of my plastomud, and my Perfectoscope will reproduce her exactly – except that this time she will be perfect. No more faults or failings. No more human error. Everyone will be perfect. Perfect husbands, perfect girlfriends. Even perfect bus drivers. I can even arrange to have one TV channel entirely devoted to Australian soap-operas. You can't ask fairer than that."

"Have you asked these people if that's what they want?" asked Willie, waving an angry hand at his frozen friends and relations.

"Why bother, dear boy? I'm so much cleverer than they are."

"I don't think you're clever at all," said Willie.

"There's no need to get on your high horse with me."

"You'll never get away with this," Willie said.

"Oh, no? Who will stop me?"

"I shall."

"I think not, dear boy. Naturally, I am totally against violence at all times. And in my perfect world there shall be none. But just at the moment, I'm afraid a little of it is called for. Claud! Cecil!"

The two Hounds stepped forward.

"I am not afraid of your digital dogs!" said Willie.

"Of course not, Prince Dingbat. You are

a Bogholler – and what Bogholler was ever afraid of anything? None of them – because none of them has enough intelligence to be afraid! But I beg you to have a care this time, dear Prince. Nothing on this earth or any other can stop these Hounds. They would happily chew up a dustbin lorry for breakfast if I asked them. You don't really want to be torn into shreds?"

"I must stop you, Uncle," said Willie. "And I shall."

"How very like a Bogholler!" said Rumpus, as he released their chains and the Hounds sprang forward and raced across the floor of the tunnel, their cold eyes fixed on Willie.

FIFTEEN

Perce Has a Brilliant Idea

Meanwhile, Perce was squinting through the knothole in the allotment gate, his sensitive ears tuned for the sound of footsteps. Samantha, head down, was gazing sadly at the iron spike that held her long rope.

"I don't like it," Perce said at last.

"It's possible he just forgot us," said Samantha.

"He wouldn't do that," said Perce. "He always brings us our titbits. I'm sure something's happened."

"Oh, dear!" said Samantha.

"Maybe he's gone down the air-shaft after that old man I told him about. Maybe he needs our help."

"What can we do?" said Samantha. "It's hopeless."

One of her big tears plopped to the ground.

"Cheer up, old friend," said Perce, turning to look at her.

She was still gazing at the spike and the rope. Percival followed the direction of her gaze.

"You've done it again, Samantha!" he said.

"Done what?"

"Pointed us in the right direction."

"Who? Me?"

"If I pulled out your spike could you leap over the fence with me on your back?"

"Easy-peasy," said Samantha. "But what good would it do?"

Percival looked from the rope and the spike to Samantha's extra-large nosebag. A pig might be lowered safely down the air-shaft in that nosebag, he thought. And the iron spike would be strong enough to take his weight.

"Prepare for the race of your life, Samantha!" he said.

SIXTEEN

Whoosh!

Willie had only a few moments to operate his remote control unit. It took him another second to aim it at the Hounds and find the right wavelength. But when he did the result was worth waiting for.

Inches away from him the slavering Hounds slid to a halt. Then, with a flick of a switch, Willie caused them to embrace one another and begin a slow tango.

"Aren't you clever!" snarled Rumpus Pundar. "Heel, Cecil! How dare you, Claud!"

The Hounds slunk towards him, thoroughly ashamed.

"Now will you depart this planet, Uncle?" said Willie.

"It seems I have no option, Prince Dingbat. But mark my words – I shall return! And when I do I shall bring my army of Indescribables!"

"That'll be nice," said Willie.

"And next time you shall not find my Hounds so easy to control!"

"I look forward to the challenge," said Willie, smiling. "At what time should we expect you?"

"When the Twin Suns of Nargar next circle the Moon of Mupp!" shrieked Rumpus. "And that time you do not know!"

"No," said Willie. "But I know a lad who does!"

"Ridiculous child!" said Rumpus, as he and his Hounds scurried along the passage to make their escape.

It took Willie only five minutes to find the WARM UP button on the Perfectoscope and switch it on. Then he went along the rows of frozen citizens activating their personal switches, all except Miss Minsky's (for whom he had other plans).

There was Wayne, the tints still in his hair and the ring still through his nose. There was his dad, his pipe still stuck in his mouth, and Councillor Allgob in his over-long overcoat and mucky flat hat.

"By gum, lad, it were colder in there than it was at that Boxing Day match against Mudchester City!" said the mayor as he sat up stiffly.

"I know not football, earthling," said Willie.

"Oh, no. I forgot, lad. Far below your standards, I expect."

Next Willie revived Shrimp – complete with his tide-mark and lug wax – and asked him when the Twin Suns of Nargar would next encircle the Moon of Mupp.

"Just a tick," said Shrimp. He consulted his watch for five minutes, during which he twice played "God Save the Queen" and once set off the beeper. "Just under an hour," he said finally.

Last of all Willie revived Sally.

"You again!" she said. "Where's that feller that were trying to freeze me to death? I won't half give him what for!"

"You will no doubt see him soon, earthen-ware child. He's gone to get his army of Indescribables. They are about to invade the earth. Canst thou walk?"

"I'll try," said Sally. Suddenly his nose caught her attention and jogged her memory at the same time. "What's happened to Willie?"

"I have given that excellent youth a secret task to perform."

"It's not one needing brains, is it?" she asked. "He's as daft as a brush."

"More courage, really," said Willie as he took her arm and led her along the tunnel. "But why dost thou keep asking after this excellent youth? Hast thou some affection for him?"

"Don't talk soft! It's just that I'll need him tomorrow night."

"Whatest for?"

"Mind your own business! When's this battle supposed to take place? I fancy a fight myself!"

"In under an hour. Could thou assemble ten tough maidens by then?"

"Easy as wink," she said. "All the maidens round here are as tough as old boots. We have to be." They'd reached the bottom of the air-shaft by now. "What the flip's that up there?" she asked. Samantha and Perce were peering down. "Those animals are trying to trap us in here!"

"I do not think so," said Willie. Putting his arms around her waist for safety purposes only he whooshed her up the air shaft.

"This is better than Blackpool!" she said.

At the top Percival and Samantha had placed the spike across the top of the air-shaft and were tying the rope to the nosebag.

"Hail, lowly creatures!" said Willie. "What art thou doing?"

"Good sir," said Perce, "my friend is about to lower me in her nosebag to the bottom of this shaft so that we can rescue a friend of ours called Willie Scrimshaw."

"Have no fear," said Willie, smiling behind his mask. "Willie Scrimshaw is safe and well and not a million miles from here."

"Then our efforts have been in vain."

"Not at all, noble creatures. There are many worthy citizens of Muckyford below. They eagerly await your rescue. Hoist them

to safety and escort them to the tip where a great battle will soon takest place — one in which I shall need your services. Now I must go to see a certain Mr Watkins. Do thou, earthenware child, assemble thy army of thy female friends within the hour. Hail and farewell!"

And he ascended into the skies.

SEVENTEEN

The Lonely Poet

Poor Mr Watkins was in his room thinking sad thoughts about Miss Minsky, and the longer the evening shadows grew the sadder grew his thoughts.

He had just taken out his love poems – all of them inspired by her – and was reading through them:

> I only have to see you
> Blow your whistle at hockey
> And my heart goes boom
> And my knees go knocky.

Could he really have written those tender and touching lines about the girl he had just been out with? It seemed impossible. And yet he *had* loved her in the distant past. Yesterday, to be exact.

He looked at another of his poems:

Dear Miss Minsky
Most wondrous of women
Life without you
Sure ain't worth livin'.

He wasn't too happy about the last line: sometimes it seemed a touch sloppy for an English teacher. Still, at least it was finished.

Unlike his latest effort, which as yet needed a final word:

Oh, Miss Minsky!
How I'd love to date her!
But she is as cold
As a – dee-dumpy-dumper

He still couldn't think how to end it. Cold shower sounded right, but didn't rhyme; alligator rhymed fine, but didn't sound right.

A sudden tapping noise made him look up. He saw a masked youth with a long nose in snazzy underpants hanging around outside his window. This rather surprised him because he lived on the third floor.

It took him some moments to realise he was looking at the Superkid from another planet who had rescued their sponsor money when thieves had tried to steal it at the Swimming Gala last term.

"What wantest thou?" he enquired. (Being an English teacher he was a dab hand at talking.) He opened the window and Willie shimmered in. "Is something amiss?"

"Verily," said Willie. "A miss is amiss!"

"I think I catch your drift," said Mr Watkins. "You mean Miss Minsky, don't you?"

"Didst thou notice something strange about her this evening?"

"I did indeed," admitted Mr Watkins, blushing the colour of a shy radish. "The warmth of her feelings made me suspect she was not the real Miss Minsky at all."

"Thou thinkest correct," said Willie. "The real Miss Minsky is in mortal danger. If you wish to save her, go to the air-shaft on the council tip where you will find a horse and a pig waiting to lower you safely down in an outsize nosebag."

"I say!" said Mr Watkins.

"When you find her, switch on her WARM UP button," continued Willie. "Once you have revived her, escort her and the other good people of Muckyford to the top of the air-shaft where in ten minutes you will witness an attempted invasion of Earth. Now I must hurry to raise an army of valiant youths to foil this attempt."

"You might try Reggie Flagg," said Mr Watkins. "He's a good fighter. And a boy called Big Wally from Bottom End. They both have gangs."

"I hope to join their gangs in one united army," said Willie.

"I'm afraid that will be impossible," said Mr Watkins.

"Nothing is impossible, Mr Watkins," said Willie, "either in war, or in love. By the way, when you find Miss Minsky, revive her with a kiss!"

And with a hiss of sparks Willie buzzed out of the window.

EIGHTEEN

Nathan Has the Wind Up

Mr Watkins was right. At first Reggie and Big Wally didn't want to join their armies together. Nothing would persuade them, they said.

But Willie had a brainwave. "By the way," he said. "I forgot to mention something. My Uncle Rumpus plans to make everybody perfect."

"Yer what?" said Reggie.

"Perfect?" said Big Wally looking goggle-eyed.

"Nobody makes me perfect!" said Reggie.

"Over my dead body!" said Big Wally.

"Then what do you suggest?" asked Willie.

Reggie and Big Wally looked at one another for a moment. Then, for the first time in history, they shook hands and smiled at one another.

Now all they were waiting for was the

enemy to turn up. Reggie's gang – which now included Nathan Peabody – manned their trenches, bows and arrows at the ready. On the other side of the tip stood Big Wally's Roman legion with their dustbin lids and broomshanks. And off to Willie's right, concealed in Hag Wood, lay his Secret Weapon.

The reporter from the *Muckyford Daily Lyre* was putting the final touches to his report on the battle minutes before it began: *In the bedlam of war on Muckyford tip tonight*, he wrote, *aliens were rubbished by local lads making good*. Behind him Mr Fletcher explained to a TV news crew how he had named Samantha after an evacuee from Liverpuddle he had fallen in love with long ago.

Close by stood the rescued citizens of Muckyford, still a little chilly in their bones but otherwise just as they always had been.

Miss Minsky and Mr Watkins had just joined them, the latter looking pleased. Not only had he awakened Miss Minsky with a kiss but also, as he gazed down at her familiar frosted features, the long-sought final word had sprung to his mind. His poem was at last complete:

> Oh, Miss Minsky!
> How I'd love to date her!
> But she is as cold
> As a refrigerator!

Near the summit of Flagg's Fort, Willie sat astride Samantha, his right hand clutching his mam's brand-new clothes prop like a lance. Samantha was hardly recognisable. Her head was up, her eyes were ready for battle. *Gallant charger, powerful warhorse*, were two of the phrases jotted down by the reporter.

By Willie's side stood his pageboy, Shrimp, holding aloft the pennant of Muckyford United. In front of him, Perce pawed the ground in anticipation.

As he pawed, bits of muck now and then fell into the rearmost trench where Nathan Peabody was crouching down quite low.

"Hast thou no stomach for the fight?" Willie kindly enquired.

"To be honest," confessed Nathan, "I'd rather play my trumpet."

"Then doest that. Take up thy stance there," said Willie. He pointed to the very top of the hill. "I will tell thee when to blow thy trumpet. Why dost thou tremble so much?"

"It's just the wind blowing up my trousers," said Nathan.

And a moment later Rumpus and his army alighted on the tip.

NINETEEN

The Battle on the Tip

It is, of course, not easy to describe the Indescribables. One or two had a hint of pirate about them. A few sported helmets with cows' horns, like the Vikings Miss Minsky had told the class about. But to Willie, most of them looked very like the things he'd seen vamoosing fast out of a carpet during a shampoo advert last week.

It was not until they were assembled in battle order that Rumpus – accompanied by his massive Hounds – dared to descend and take up his position in the very centre.

Then Willie called down from the top of the tip, "Rumpus Pundar! I charge thee and thy evil hordes to depart this planet!"

"Phooey!" said his uncle.

Once more Willie warned him, but Rumpus merely laughed.

"So be it!" said Willie. He raised aloft his mam's new clothes prop, gave Nathan the signal to blow his trumpet, and shouted: "Let battle commence!"

At once Reggie's army whanged down a load of wellies and their dads' smelly socks filled with mud and worse. After that they fired their arrows, most of which veered off over the allotments. Roars of laughter erupted from the ranks of the evil Indescribables. But their laughter was short-lived. Willie had cunningly ordered the archers to fire off-target and the arrows, after completing a circle, winged back to strike terror into the backsides of the enemy.

Then Willie heaved Shrimp up into the saddle behind him and urged Samantha to charge downhill. One trench she jumped, two, and a third. Inside she was thinking, *Not quite the Grand National, but beggars can't be choosers*. A moment later they burst through the massed ranks of the Indescribables who were still extracting arrows from their sensitive parts. Willie swept

hundreds of them aside with his mam's clothes prop. Perce, thundering alongside, did unmentionable damage down below.

Willie drew rein when they had reached Big Wally.

"Ready, Legionary Wally?"

"Ready!" said Big Wally.

Then Shrimp dismounted, strode bravely to the front and held his pennant high: "Hail, Muckyford United!" he cried aloud.

At the second blast of Nathan's trumpet,

Big Wally's men began a slow march forward. They looked full of menace with their binlids on their left arms, their broom-shanks bristling in anger.

The Indescribables fought well consider-ing most still had arrows attached to their bottoms. Their huge swords whistled above their heads as they sang their warcry – which Willie noticed was entirely composed of four-letter words. Their pong was really honky, for they were the sort who rarely washed their undies. Some even had hor-rible tattoos on them like, *I luv my darling muvver*. But nothing could stop Big Wally's legion following Shrimp's standard and they bashed their way through till they reached Flagg's Fort and the two armies were united.

Willie looked down on the Indescribables. A lot of them were talking about going away and coming back a week next Tuesday. One chap was muttering about danger money. Another felt an urge to visit his Aunty Vera.

But most of them were still game to fight.

It was time to introduce Willie's Secret Weapon. He ordered the last blast of the trumpet. Almost before Nathan's trembling lips had squeezed out his first note, Sally and her pals burst out of Hag Wood like a bunch of screaming nutters.

Among them was Brenda Slack, whose hobby was squashing people flat at play-time. And Lucy Fidgit, a dainty girl with a black belt in karate. Lots of them whirled their mothers' handbags and brandished rolling-pins. Sally had her grandma's hat-pin. It was six inches long.

There were only eleven girls but they soon made mincemeat of the poor Indescribables. Brenda Slack was squashing them flat. Little Lucy was felling them like ninepins, screaming *Haachee!* and *Haachoo!* and the other things that karate people say. Every time Sally struck home with her grandma's hatpin there was a loud POP and an Indescribable burst into smelly shreds.

In no time at all they were a defeated rabble. Some were on their knees, begging for mercy. Four of them proposed to Brenda Slack but she turned them all down and sat on them instead.

"Now will ye depart?" asked Willie in a highly heroic tone of voice.

"Certainly!" shouted the Indescribables.

"Never!" cried Rumpus Pundar.

"In that case, you're on your own!"

shouted the Indescribables.

"Cowards!" shrieked Rumpus Pundar. "Backsliders!"

"Those girls don't fight fair!" shouted the Indescribables.

"In that case you've lost your bonus payments!" said Uncle Rumpus.

"Stuff your bonus payments!" shouted the Indescribables.

And a moment later they had gone.

It did not surprise Willie that Uncle Rumpus was still smiling. He knew what a devious mind his uncle had. Nor did it surprise him when he bent down and unleashed the Hounds of Gobbolot.

"See if you can stop them this time, Prince Dingbat!" hissed his uncle. "Seek, Claud! Kill, Cecil!"

The Hounds streaked across the tip towards Willie. The combined army of Sally, Reggie and Wally fought hard but it was not weirdo warriors with sweaty armpits they were up against now. This time it was machines. It was robots.

Willie fiddled with his remote control unit, trying this wavelength and that.

But the Hounds came on and on.

He knew that he must stop them. If he failed, it would be Muckyford today, and tomorrow the world. After that, they would probably conquer the universe.

When the Hounds reached the top of the hill and confronted him, Willie tossed aside his useless control unit and stepped down from the saddle. He laid his mam's new clothes prop carefully on the ground (she'd have played heck if he'd broken it), and advanced towards the Hounds.

"We meet again, dear boy," said Cecil, showing his needle teeth.

"Prepare to meet thy doom!" sniggered Claud.

Willie could have escaped, of course. He could have flown away. But that sort of thing isn't in an Obsblud's blood. Instead, he delivered a huge punch on Cecil's jaw.

"Do you know, Claud," said Cecil. "I think a gnat just stung me."

It seemed like the end for Willie.

But it wasn't.

A long, low growl sounded from below them on the tip.

Looking down, Willie saw Mr Longstaff's lurcher.

Miss Minsky had told them that dogs were related to wolves, and many moons ago dogs had sprung from the ancient wolfpacks. It was possible that Oscar's great-granddad hadn't sprung very far.

Certainly Oscar had a very wolfy look about him. His eyes glowed, his hair bristled, and even as they watched he put back his head and gave a long, wolfy howl.

You must try to imagine the thoughts that were going through Oscar's mind as he hurtled up the slope. For two years he'd been prowling the streets hoping to come across a single dog to fight, without success. They had all avoided him. And here were two dogs, before his very eyes. And big dogs, too, which made it even better.

Oscar was five feet off the ground when he hit Cecil on the snoot. His eyes were almost as big as the Hounds', and red with an ancient anger. One of his ears came off quite early, followed by several parts of his tail and a small piece from somewhere I'd rather not mention. But Oscar fought on.

If the truth be known, he probably quite enjoyed losing ears and things. The Hounds battled grimly, coldly, mechanically. But their hearts weren't in it, not like Oscar's. Willie was lost in admiration for this brave and noble beast as more and more bits of him came off.

Willie decided to join in. Soon he was followed by Sally and most of the rest. When Oscar gnashed through Cecil's essential wiring, sparks started coming out of the great Hound's ears. When he rushed Claud from the rear he accidentally loosened the pink ribbon that secured the battery case and Claud's batteries tumbled out behind him and he came to a stuttering halt. A minute later a white hand – Nathan's, for he was the only one who had not joined in – reached up from deep down in a trench and pulled Cecil's ribbon so that *his* batteries also fell out. Cecil's eyes gave a final wrong-way spin. Then he, too, juddered to a halt. And the battle was over.

"Now will ye depart, Uncle?" called Willie from his height.

But his uncle had already departed.

All they could see of him was a cloud of dirty yellow dust that spiralled upwards accompanied by melancholy laughter.

"Well done, Oscar," said Willie.

"Yes!" everybody shouted. "Well done, Oscar!"

Oscar wagged his tail, once.

Then he went off to look for another fight.

TWENTY

Dirt Beneath His Fingernails

It was all in the *Muckyford Daily Lyre* the following evening.

"By gum, Mother!" said Mr Scrimshaw, puffing smoke. "I'm glad I were there. It says Shrimp Salmon's going to get the Allgob Medal for Valour in the field."

"I thought it was on the tip," said Mrs Scrimshaw, happily chopping up chips in the kitchen. "And where were you all this time, Our Willie?"

"Doing me project, Mam, upstairs."

"Just as well. I don't want you getting them new boots mucky."

"It says here, Mother, that Superkid swept away the alien hordes as if they were dirt beneath his fingernails," said Mr Scrimshaw.

"It's marvellous what that Superkid can do," replied Mrs Scrimshaw. "But he shouldn't have dirt beneath his fingernails.

That's not right."

"There's a photo of him in the paper, Mother, with his lance. Come and have a look."

"Oh, that's a lance, is it?" she said, peering over his shoulder and nearly slicing his ear with her tatie knife. "It looks very like my new clothes prop."

"By gum! You're right, Mother. And while you're on about it, that Superkid's nose fair reminds me of somebody."

Willie, sitting next to him on their busted sofa, hid his nose deeper in his scampi and vinegar crisp packet.

"You're quite right. Whoever can it be, Albert?"

"I've a feeling it's somebody we know, Mother. Somebody close."

It was just a lucky thing that Darleen came in at that moment, smiling all over her face.

"Guess where Wayne is, Mam?" she said. "In Tan-U-Fast, getting brown all over! And tonight we're having a Kangaroo Lager party!"

"It is nice when things get back to normal!" said Mrs Scrimshaw.

"What about his tints?" asked Mr Scrimshaw.

"I'm highlighting them tonight," said Darleen, "after we've practised our tango."

Willie smiled to himself. Everything was working out champion. Reggie Flagg's gang and Big Wally's were going to play football on the tip every Saturday instead of fighting over it. The allotments were saved because the council had put Rumpus's "perfect" plastomud people on exhibition and money was rolling in – folk were flooding in from as far as Posset Bottom. The Hounds of Gobbolot were to be erected outside the Town Hall under the Roman motto, *Labore Omnia Vincit*, which roughly translated means Labour Always Wins. Last but not least, only five minutes ago Willie's dad had asked him for the lend of five bob. So everything was back to normal.

There was only one thing worrying Willie.

He still hadn't asked Sally to go to the disco with him.

And at that moment there was a knock on their back door.

TWENTY-ONE

Happy Ending

By coincidence it was Sally Mow.

"Hello, Mrs Scrimshaw," she said. "Can I borrow your Willie?"

"You can have him permanently, as far as we're concerned, Sal!" said Darleen. "What do you want him for?"

"He's taking me to the school disco."

"Am I, Sal?" Willie asked as she came in the room.

He'd never seen her looking so nice: she had a ribbon in her hair and her ankle socks were that white they nearly knocked his eyes out.

"Well, I can't go by meself, can I?" said Sally.

"He never had any gumption, Sal," said Darleen. "Don't stand there like a petrified beetroot, Our Willie. Get yourself upstairs and get changed. How's your mum and the baby, Sally?"

*

Upstairs, Willie put on his Muckyford United football shirt and looked at himself in the wardrobe mirror: he didn't look bad if he half-closed his eyes. He glanced down at his fingernails. There *was* dirt underneath them. He'd have to get that out before his mam twigged.

Outside it was a lovely evening, hardly raining at all, spuggies chirruping away in the roof-gutters. It made you feel glad to be alive. Halfway down Balaclava Street they saw Mr Fletcher come out of Number 46 with a bucket of pigswill in one hand and a nice-looking old lady holding on to the other.

"Who's that?" asked Willie.

"Samantha."

"It can't be, Sally," said Willie. "Samantha's a h—"

"The *real* Samantha, you lummock! When she saw the news on the telly she got the train from Liverpuddle straight away. She's never forgotten Mr Fletcher. They're getting married next week." She looked at Willie for a moment. "I wish I knew somebody like that with a bit of gumption!"

"What do you mean, Sal?"

"Who did you think was going to take me to the disco, Willie Scrimshaw?"

"I thought you might prefer Nathan Peabody. Somebody wi' principles."

"He sharp forgot his principles about not fighting when Knocker Bowles shoved his fist under his nose," said Sally. "He signed on for Reggie Flagg's gang straight away. Not like somebody I know."

"How do you mean, Sal?"

"Somebody I know got walloped three times by Knocker Bowles in the playground the other day, and never wavered once."

"I never knew you saw that."

"I'm not as daft as I look, Willie Scrimshaw. I were right proud of you that day. That's what I call real principles."

"Is that what principles are, Sal?" said Willie. "I never knew that."

"There's not a lot you do know, my lad!"

"But I'm not a virtu-whatsit like Nathan."

"You mean he can blow his own trumpet?"

"*And* he's right good at sums, Sal."

"He still doesn't add up to much."

"And you think I do?" said Willie as they entered the school yard.

"I never said that. Don't get above yourself, Scrimshaw."

"But you do like me?"

"I wish you wouldn't talk soft!"

As they passed the school kitchen they saw Mr Watkins and Miss Minsky making fruit juice together for the disco. Miss Minsky almost smiled as he leaned down and gave her what might have been a kiss, only a bit of net curtain got in the way.

"But you do think I'm all right, Sally?" asked Willie as they went into the hall.

"I'll be honest with you, Willie. You're little and skinny with a nose bigger than a budgie's, but as far as I can make out you're the best thing on offer round here, so give us your hand."

"What for, Sal?"

"The Birdy Song's just starting. I reckon that should suit you! Come on, you big dollop! And try not to look so gormless!"

And she dragged him into the dance.